Witness

by David Belbin

Series Editors: Steve Barlow and Steve Skidmore

Published by Heinemann Educational Publishers
Halley Court, Jordan Hill, Oxford OX2 8EJ
A division of Reed Educational and Professional Publishing Ltd

OXFORD   MELBOURNE   AUCKLAND
JOHANNESBURG   BLANTYRE   GABORONE
IBADAN   PORTSMOUTH NH (USA)   CHICAGO

05   04   03   02   01
10   9   8   7   6   5   4   3   2   1
ISBN 0 435 21507 8

Illustrations by Andrew Skilleter
Cover design by Shireen Nathoo Design
Designed by Artistix, Thame, Oxon
Printed and bound in Great Britain by Athenaeum Press Ltd

Tel: 01865 888058   www.heinemann.co.uk

Contents

CHAPTER 1

Liam was late, thanks to an after-school detention. His short-cut home took him through The Ramble. Most people stayed away from The Ramble after dark. It was badly lit. People got mugged there, and worse.

The Ramble might be run-down but parts of it were busy. There were plenty of people in the *Dover Castle* pub. The nightclub next door was boarded up.

A slim man stepped out of its shadowy doorway and hissed. 'Looking for something?'

He meant drugs. Liam hurried along, ignoring him. There was some kind of fight further up the street, so Liam crossed to the other side. If there was one rule in The Ramble, it was this: don't get involved.

Liam couldn't help looking at the fight.

Across the road, a tall Asian man tumbled to the ground. Had he been stabbed? Liam didn't want to know. The man's attacker was in shadow. Liam couldn't see him properly and he didn't want to. This wasn't his business. Head down, he walked on quickly.

The attacker ran across the street ahead of Liam. As he did, a car came out of a side street with its lights on. Liam didn't mean to, but he got a good look at the attacker. He was white, with a shaved head, a square jaw and deep-set eyes. The attacker slipped a knife inside his jacket and smiled to himself.

A moment later, he was gone. Had the attacker noticed him? Liam couldn't say. It didn't matter. Liam wasn't going to tell anybody what he'd seen. He wasn't going to go back to check on the victim, either. Somebody might see him.

Should he find a phone and call an ambulance? No. The man was sure to have a friend who would help him out. This wasn't Liam's business. Also, if he didn't get home soon, there'd be nothing left for dinner.

CHAPTER 2

The bus to school next morning took Liam past The Ramble. He was surprised to see police notices everywhere. They were on shop windows and doorways, tied to lamp-posts and railings.

MURDER! TUESDAY, ABOUT 6PM

There was a photo with the words 'Did you see this man?' Liam couldn't see the face properly. But it didn't matter. He hadn't seen the victim. So he was dead. Liam didn't see what the big fuss was about. There was a murder every few months in The Ramble. The police didn't usually go to town with posters like this.

At the next stop, his friend Matt got on.

'What's this about a murder last night?' Liam asked Matt.

'Some drug thing, I expect,' Matt said. 'They got the posters up quick, didn't they?'

Matt lived in a street near The Ramble, above his dad's betting shop.

'I think I saw it,' Liam whispered to Matt. He explained how he came to be in The Ramble.

'You really saw the killer?' Matt asked, in a hushed voice.

'Maybe,' Liam said. 'I didn't mean to.'

'I'd keep quiet about that if I were you,' said Matt.

'I will,' Liam replied. 'In fact, forget I told you about it.'

'About what?' Matt asked and they both laughed.

Liam thought that would be the end of it. On the way home, he didn't look at the posters of the murdered man. When he got in, however, the evening paper was on the table.

'DEATH OF A LOCAL HERO!' screamed the headline. 'City Councillor murdered in The Ramble.'

Liam read the story. It said that Mohammed Khan was on a mission to clean up The Ramble. He was fighting to drive out drug dealers, guns and working girls. But he had been sent death threats.

The story went on, 'Khan was knifed at around 6pm. He was returning from a meeting to discuss a new youth centre in The Ramble. His body was not found until about six-thirty, by which time he had bled to death.'

Liam felt terrible. If he had gone to help Khan, he might still be alive. All Liam had needed to do was dial 999. But he hadn't cared what happened to Khan. Now Khan was dead.

Liam got changed, then left the house.

'Are you going for fish and chips?' his brother, Ben, called after him. 'Will you get me some?'

Liam didn't reply. He didn't know where he was going. He wasn't a grass. He didn't want to get involved, but he was involved. He'd seen the killer. He could remember every detail of the man's face.

He walked around town, thinking. If he reported what he'd seen, some people would hate him. Others would say that he'd done the right thing. Either way, things would never be the same again. Liam found himself outside the central police station. He couldn't decide whether or not to go in.

CHAPTER 3

Liam walked into the police station.

'It's about the councillor who got killed,' he told the sergeant at the desk. She looked at him coldly.

'Come to give yourself up, have you?' she asked.

'I saw it happen,' Liam told her, in a quiet voice.

'Pull the other one,' the desk sergeant said. 'I know your type. You're a time-waster.'

'I saw who did it,' Liam growled angrily.

The desk sergeant saw that he was serious. 'Hold on,' she said. 'I'll call the incident room.'

Five minutes later, Liam was talking to a senior officer from CID.

'Describe the man you saw.'

'Medium height. Shaved head. Deep-set eyes.'

'Would you know him again?'

'I should think so,' Liam replied.

They asked him to look through books full of mugshots. So this was what it felt like to be a grass. Suddenly, he spotted him.

'That's the man!' he told the officer with him.

'Are you sure?' the CID man asked.

'Positive,' Liam told him.

The officer rushed out of the room. Minutes later, Liam was being questioned again. This time it was by the officer in charge, Detective Superintendent Wright.

'It was brave of you to come forward,' the Superintendent said. 'It can't have been easy.'

'Save the soft soap,' Liam told him. 'I want to get this over with. What else do you need to know?'

Once more, he went through everything he had seen. Detective Superintendent Wright thanked him. Then he asked Liam to leave by a back entrance.

'Don't tell anybody that you've been to see us, not even your family. If this comes to court and the killer pleads not guilty, you're going to need protection.'

Liam said nothing. Five minutes later, he was out on the street. He'd missed his dinner, but it didn't matter. He wasn't hungry.

'Where've you been?' Ben asked when he got in.

'Nowhere,' Liam replied and turned on the television.

Khan's murder was the lead story on the local news. They said that the councillor had been trying to get the old nightclub knocked down. He wanted a youth centre there instead. A reporter spoke to Khan's wife.

'My husband was a good and a brave man,' she said. 'He has paid a terrible price for his bravery.'

Liam wondered what price he would have to pay.

CHAPTER 4

'Did you hear what happened last night?'
Matt asked Liam on the bus to school.

'No. What?'

'They arrested Danny Reece for killing
that Asian councillor.'

'You're kidding!'

Liam knew who Danny Reece was. Reece
and his gang more or less owned The Ramble.
Their base was the old nightclub.

'What does Danny Reece look like?' he
asked.

'Hard,' Matt replied. 'He's got a shaved
head.'

'How old is he?' Liam wanted to know.

'Thirty-five, forty. Was he the bloke you
saw?'

'Don't know,' Liam replied. But now he

knew why the police were so excited when he picked out the photo. They had been after Danny Reece for years.

'He uses my dad's betting shop,' Matt went on. 'That's how I know him. Danny only goes out after dark. You didn't tell anyone what you saw, did you?'

'No,' Liam lied, 'of course not. Did you?'

'What do you think I am?' Matt replied angrily.

He hadn't actually denied it, Liam realised later.

Danny Reece's arrest was all over the evening paper that night. The paper showed a very old photo of the gang boss. Yet Liam was sure it was him, all right.

'The police will not confirm or deny that they have a witness to the stabbing,' the paper said.

Liam swore. Matt had better keep his mouth shut. If he didn't, Liam's life was worth less than dog meat. It was said that Reece had murdered more than once before. But the police had never had a witness … until now.

That night, Liam stayed at home. Next morning, he got an early bus to school in case anyone was looking for him. At school, Matt avoided Liam. Liam went to sit with him at lunch, but Matt blanked him. He must have worked out that Liam was the police witness. The question was, had Matt told anyone?

The answer became clear as Liam was walking home from the bus stop. In broad daylight, on the main road, a white van pulled up in front of Liam. Its back doors flew open. Two hooded men jumped out. They grabbed Liam, dragged him into the van and gave him a beating.

'You're the grass that got Danny Reece taken in.'

A heavy boot hit him in the stomach.

One of the hooded men whispered in his ear.

'This is what you've got to do. Tell the police it was dark, you're not sure who you saw. Understand?'

Liam nodded. With a screech of brakes, the van came to a halt. Liam was thrown out onto the road.

He didn't know where he was until his mum and brother came out. They carried him into the house.

'Liam! What happened?' Mum asked. He had to tell her now.

'I was the witness. I had no choice.'

His mum didn't look convinced.

CHAPTER 5

Liam was off school for a week. When he went back, all the hard lads at school treated him like dirt. He couldn't walk from one class to another without being kicked. After a day, his ankles were covered in bruises.

Teachers saw what was going on, but didn't help him. Even his brother, Ben, thought Liam was mad. Why was he risking his life, for some Asian he didn't know?

The police had Liam in to go over his statement.

'I can't take this any more,' Liam said. 'I want to withdraw my statement.'

'How will that change things?' Detective Superintendent Wright asked. 'The first chance he gets, Reece will have you killed.'

'Why?' Liam wanted to know.

'As revenge for turning him in. And because you might change your mind. It's too late to go back now. Look, why don't you let us move you to a safe house?'

'I'll think about it,' Liam said.

That night, he had a visitor. It was Matt. His friend hadn't been to Liam's house since before the murder.

'We need to talk,' Matt said. 'I want to help.'

'Help?' Liam said. 'You told Reece who I was!'

Matt replied. 'And you lied to me about going to the police. Danny's a friend of my dad. He saw you in The Ramble. He asked me about somebody there in school uniform. I told him because there was money in it for you. Then I found out you'd already been to the police. I never thought you were a grass.'

'He murdered that councillor in cold blood!' Liam argued.

'What do you know?' Matt replied. 'Maybe the guy deserved it. Anyway, I've been sent to offer you a sweetener.'

'What for?' Liam asked.

'Don't withdraw your statement. Go to court. Then, when you're in the witness box, say you're no longer sure what happened. It was a dark night. The guy who did the stabbing looked a lot younger than Danny. There's thirty grand in it for you, if Danny gets off.'

'I'd be done for perjury!' Liam argued.

'No, you wouldn't. Say the police forced you into testifying. They can't prove anything. Plus, the jury's on our side. The fix is in. Know what I mean?'

'I understand,' Liam said, 'but I'd be a criminal.'

'If you don't do it,' Matt said, 'you'll be dead!'

After he'd gone, Liam tried to decide what to do. He struggled with himself, but it all came to the same thing. There was right and there was wrong. Once you went wrong, you couldn't go back. No amount of money would buy you a good night's sleep.

But there was another problem. From what Matt had said, it sounded like some of the jury had been bribed. So Reece was bound to get off. If Liam did what the gang leader wanted, he could still make a lot of money. Whereas, if he told the truth, it might not make any difference. Liam didn't know what to do.

CHAPTER 6

In court, the prosecution said that Reece was an evil man.

'He's got away with murder many times because there's never been a witness. But now we have one.'

The defence argued that all of this was rubbish.

'Danny Reece is a community leader. He is a well-respected man. Mohammed Khan was himself a drug dealer. He used his position on the council as a cover.

'Khan was also a violent man. He carried a knife at all times. The defence does not know how he died. It was probably a fight which he lost. But we do know that Danny Reece did not stab him. We have a dozen witnesses who will swear that he was with

them at the time. Danny Reece has no case
to answer.'

Liam was confused by all of this. The police had warned him that Reece would have a fake alibi. But what if these stories about the councillor were true?

If Khan was a crook, why was Liam risking his life to put Reece in prison? As the trial went on, it got harder and harder to see the truth.

'Khan was a saint,' said the Council leader. 'If anyone could clean up The Ramble, he was the man.'

Liam found it hard to sleep at night. He wanted to tell the truth. But even if he did, Danny Reece was likely to get off. However, if Liam lied a little, he would be safe. He could go home. He might even get thirty thousand pounds. All he had to do was tell one tiny fib: 'I thought it was him. Now I'm not so sure.'

A barrister went over Liam's statement with him.

'The jury can tell when people are lying,' she said. 'They've a good idea that Danny Reece bribed people to say bad things about Khan. But they'll know that you have no reason to lie. They'll believe you.'

Liam wasn't so sure. The night before he was due to testify, his mum and brother came to see him.

'Things are bad at school,' Ben said. 'I keep getting threats. If you say Reece did it, it's not just you who will have to move away. None of us will be safe.'

'Do what you have to do,' Mum told Liam. 'But think about this. Danny Reece has a very strong alibi. It was dark and you'd never seen him before. Are you a hundred per cent sure that it was him?'

'I'm only sure of one thing,' Liam answered. 'Tomorrow morning, I'll be in the witness box.'

CHAPTER 7

The courtroom was crowded. Danny Reece
looked confident. The jury seemed tired and
fed up. The two youngest jurors did not look
Liam in the face. Were they the ones who
Reece had bribed?

Liam glanced at the public gallery. There
was Matt. His friend made a slitting
movement across his throat. If Liam didn't
lie, he was a dead man.

The prosecution began its questioning.
'Please describe what you saw that night.'
Liam said exactly what he'd seen.
'Is the man you saw in this room today?'
Liam turned to look at Reece. He opened
his mouth. No words came out. He coughed.
'I can't...' He felt sick. Faces in the
courtroom spun around him. Suddenly, Liam

fell to the floor.

When Liam came to, he was in the judge's rooms.

'Are you well enough to continue, Liam?'

'Not really,' Liam told the judge. 'I'm terrified.'

'You'd better tell me why,' the judge said.

Liam told her about the threats and the bribed jury.

'You don't surprise me,' the judge said. 'The police warned me that this was likely to happen.'

Back in court, the judge explained that Liam had withdrawn his testimony, so she was stopping the trial.

'The charges will remain on file, but there isn't enough evidence. You're free to go,' she told Reece.

There was cheering. Most of the jurors looked relieved. So did Matt, Ben and Liam's mum.

That night, on The Ramble, there were loud parties. Thanks to Liam, Danny Reece was a free man.

The following day, Matt came to see Liam at home.

'You did a great job in court,' he said, handing Liam a brown envelope. 'Here's thirty grand. Danny says, "Be careful, don't flash the money around".'

'Don't worry,' Liam said, 'I won't spend it, yet.'

'We weren't sure about you for a while there,' Matt told him. 'Danny almost had you killed.'

'I was stupid,' Liam admitted. 'I should have taken the money as soon as you offered it. By the way, how much did the jurors get?'

'Ten grand each. But, they weren't needed, after all.'

'It was the youngest ones, wasn't it?' asked Liam.

'Probably,' Matt said. 'I wouldn't know.'

'But I would,' Liam told him. 'You see, the police arrested them, half an hour ago.'

In a panic, Matt stood up. Before he could get to the door, the police were in the room. They handcuffed him.

'There's going to be a new trial,' Liam told Matt. 'Only this time, it'll be a hundred miles away, with a new jury. And most of Reece's gang will be on trial too. For bribery and perjury, amongst other things.

'The only question is, will you be with them? If you tell the truth, you might get off with a warning. So now it's your turn to sweat. What are you going to do, Matt?'

Before Matt could think of what to say, the police took him away.